SACRAMENTO PUBLIC LIBRARY
828 "I" Street
Sacramento, CA 95814
11/19

D0116296

Translated from the French *Hôtel Bellevie*

First published in the United Kingdom in 2019
by Thames & Hudson Ltd, 181A High Holborn,
London WC1V 7QX

www.thamesandhudson.com

First published in the United States of America
in 2019 by Thames & Hudson Inc.,
500 Fifth Avenue, New York, New York 10110

www.thamesandhudsonusa.com

Original edition © 2018 Éditions Sarbacane, Paris
This edition © 2019 Thames & Hudson Ltd, London

English translation rights arranged through La Petite Agence, Paris

All Rights Reserved. No part of this publication may be reproduced
or transmitted in any form or by any means, electronic or mechanical,
including photocopy, recording or any other information storage and
retrieval system, without prior permission in writing from the publisher.

British Library Cataloguing-in-Publication Data
A catalogue record for this book is available from the British Library

Library of Congress Control Number 2019931893

ISBN 978-0-500-65212-1

Printed and bound in Malaysia

HERRING HOTEL

SERGE BLOCH

DIDIER LÉVY

Thames & Hudson

My parents own a hotel by the sea. Once it was called the Sherrington Hotel, but some of the letters fell off the sign, so now it's called the Herring Hotel. The building is very old and a bit crumbly. In fact, it's falling apart.

Every morning before I go to school, I help to fetch tea and coffee for the guests. The breakfast room has so many holes in the ceiling that we've put buckets all over the floor, to catch the drips when it rains.

Our guests are a funny bunch. Most of them have been living here for years. I suppose we've become like a family to them.

There's Mr. Folds, who always sits at the same table. He spends his time making paper animals and birds, which he leaves all over the hotel. There's Mr. Kipp, who walks in his sleep. He often wanders down the corridors at the oddest times. There's Madame Lafleur, who is French and very elegant. She never takes off her sunglasses. There are the Molotov twins, who love to play chess. They always look grumpy. And there's Mr. Babacan, who's a chef. He works at the best kebab house in town.

And there, at the back of the breakfast room, is Mrs. Kettle. She's quite something. She always wears a blue housecoat, shiny gold slippers, lots of red lipstick, and a big crown on her head.

I smile and say "Coffee, Mrs. Kettle?"

She stares at me sternly. "Please show a little respect, Gabriel! You're talking to Tina the 23rd, exiled Queen of Kettlippia!"

"I'm terribly sorry, Your Majesty. Would you like some coffee, Your Queenliness?"

"That's much better," she says. "I would love a cup."

Pointing to an apple on the table, she asks "Could you peel this for me, Gabriel?" I peel it carefully, and cut it into four quarters. Mrs. Kettle rummages in her bag and pulls out a medal.

"For loyal service to Tina the 23rd, exiled Queen of Kettlippia, I pronounce you a Knight of the Order of the Pelican!"

As it happens, I have lots of medals already. When I chased a wasp out of Mrs. Kettle's room, she gave me a medal. When I bought her some polish for her crown, she gave me a medal. And best of all, the medals are made of chocolate. Delicious!

Mrs. Kettle and I like to walk on the beach together. She tells me lots of stories about Kettlippia. It's a very small country. In fact, it's so tiny that it's not included on many maps. In summer, butterflies from all over the world go there for a big party. In winter, bears from all over the world go there for a big snowball fight.

Mrs. Kettle grew up in a palace by the sea. The palace walls were made of glass, so everyone could watch the pelicans outside. And when she became queen, there was a huge crowd of them waiting to cheer for her. Hundreds and hundreds of pelicans!

But one day, the tiny country of Kettlippia was invaded by an army from the big country next door. Mrs. Kettle had to jump on a motorbike and leave Kettlippia behind. That was thirty-seven years ago.

I love hearing stories about Kettlippia. Sometimes I feel as if I grew up there myself.

My parents like Mrs. Kettle, but they don't understand her like I do. "You shouldn't believe everything she tells you, you know," my mother tells me.

"She's a little bit crazy," my father agrees. "You must have noticed." Then he steps back to make way for Mr. Kipp the sleepwalker, who comes wandering through the room.

"What do you think, Gabriel?" my mother asks.

"Maybe she's a bit unusual," I reply. "But I don't care. Mrs. Kettle's my friend and I like her!" Suddenly there's a loud and terrible CRASH!

We rush outside. One of the hotel walls has fallen down! The water coming through the roof must have made it crumble. Soon the Molotov twins arrive, followed by Mr. Babacan and Madame Lafleur.

"Nothing to worry about!" my dad says with his biggest smile. "It's just a spot of bad weather. You can all go back to your rooms. Everything's fine. Absolutely fine!"

But our guests aren't stupid. They can see how bad the damage is. So the next morning we all roll up our sleeves and start moving the rubble. Everyone helps us in their own way. One of the Molotov twins moves the black pieces of rubble, and the other twin moves the white pieces. Mr. Babacan wraps up each piece of rubble like one of his kebabs. And Mr. Folds tries to turn his pieces into animals.

The only person who doesn't do anything is Mrs. Kettle. She doesn't speak. She doesn't even eat her breakfast.

"What's wrong, Your Majesty?" I ask.

"It's all over," she sighs. "Everything's falling to pieces, I know it. It's just like when I left Kettlippia." And she tells me her story all over again.

Then she looks at me for a moment and smiles. "You probably think I'm a little bit crazy, Gabriel," she says. "Everyone thinks I'm a little bit crazy. But I want you to know that I'm very fond of you. And I would love it if you called me Granny."

I don't know what to say. There's a big lump in my throat. So I just hold her hand. Her warm and wrinkled hand.

Suddenly there's another huge CRASH. Another part of the hotel has fallen down!

My parents gather everyone together in the dining room. Water is pouring through the cracks in the ceiling. My mother speaks first.

"Ladies and gentlemen! As you can see, the place is falling down around us. We must leave the Herring Hotel right away! Pack your things quickly, and thank you so much for being such wonderful guests."

Two hours later, we're all standing outside, next to a big heap of suitcases and boxes. It's almost time to say goodbye. Everybody is trying not to cry, and not hiding it very well. Madame Lafleur has taken off her sunglasses and Mr. Kipp is wide awake for once. The Molotov twins gaze sadly at what's left of the hotel, while Mrs. Kettle gives out medals to everyone for being brave.

Then Mr. Babacan calls out to us. He's spotted something coming down the road. It's a long line of cars, driving very slowly.

"They're coming to our hotel," my dad says.

"We can't take new guests!" my mother sobs. "We'll have to tell them to leave."

My dad is right. The cars are coming our way. They park right next to the pile of rubble where our hotel used to be.

People begin to get out of the cars. Dozens of them. Hundreds of them. Thousands of them! As we watch in amazement, the crowd starts to shout. "Your Majesty! The kingdom of Kettlippia is free once more! We've come to take you home to the land where you belong!"

Queen Tina the 23rd of Kettlippia, also known as Mrs. Kettle, smiles an enormous smile.

"At last!" she sighs. "I've waited so long!"

Then Her Majesty comes over to speak to my parents and the other guests. She has an important question to ask them. Can you guess what it is?

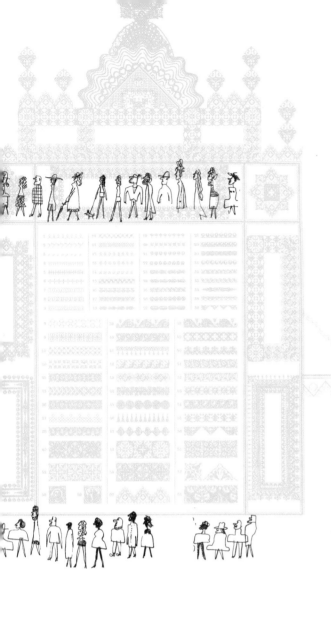

The Herring Hotel, every little bit of it, is shipped all the way to Kettlippia. And by the sea, right next door to the palace with glass walls, we rebuild it. Mr. Folds, Mr. Kipp, Madame Lafleur, Mr. Babacan and the Molotov twins help us in every way they can.

As for the Queen of Kettlippia and I, we go for walks on the beach together every day and look at the pelicans. And of course, I call her Granny. Or Granny Tina. Or Her Royal Granniness.

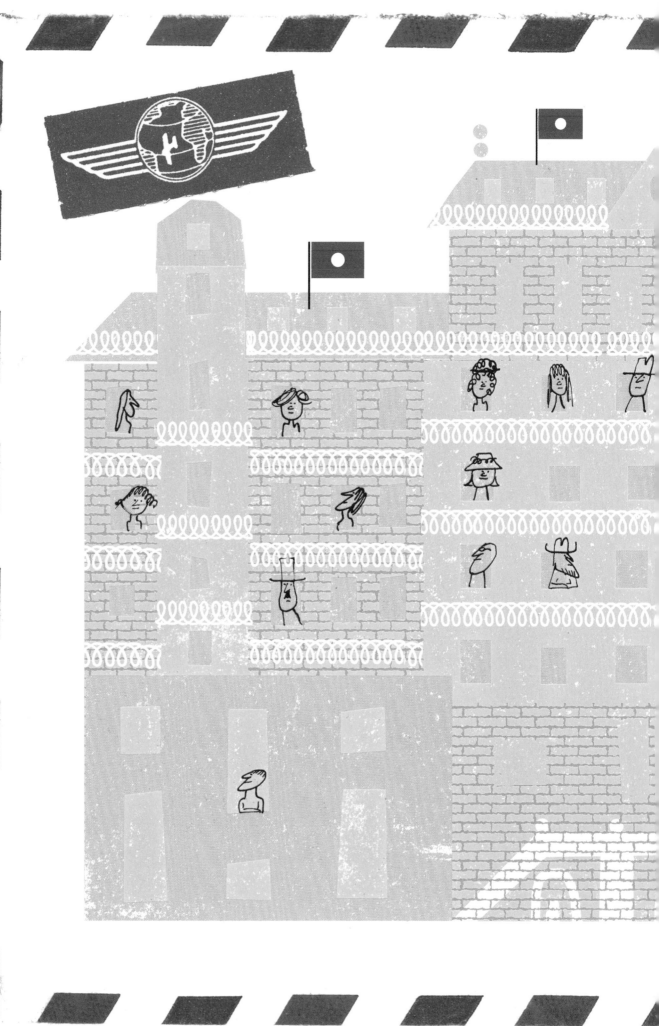

Kettlippia is a lovely little country. And if you'd like to visit one day,
I know the name of an excellent hotel…

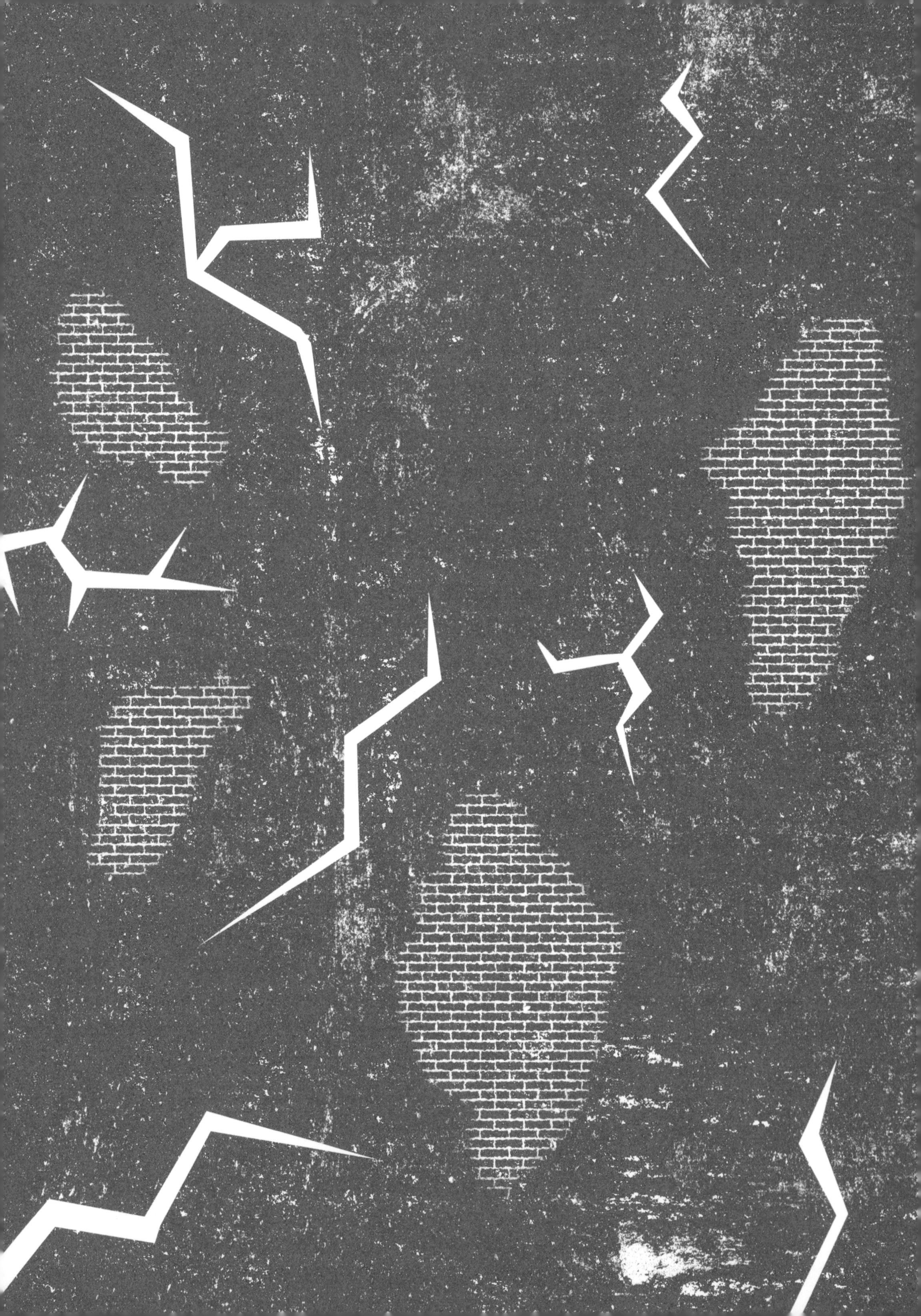